I'll Always Love You

By HANS WILHELM

Dragonfly Books ———✦ New York

To Lea

All rights reserved. Published in the United States by Dragonfly Books, an imprint of Random House Children's Books, a division of Random House, Inc., New York. Originally published in hardcover in the United States by Crown Publishers, Inc., a division of Random House, Inc., New York, in 1985.

Dragonfly Books with the colophon is a registered trademark of Random House, Inc.

Visit us on the Web! www.randomhouse.com/kids

Educators and librarians, for a variety of teaching tools, visit us at www.randomhouse.com/teachers

Library of Congress Cataloging-in-Publication Data
Wilhelm, Hans.
I'll always love you / by Hans Wilhelm.
     p.   cm.
Summary: A child's sadness at the death of a beloved dog is tempered by the remembrance of saying to it every night, "I'll always love you."
ISBN 978-0-517-55648-1 (hardcover) — ISBN 978-0-517-57759-2 (lib. bdg.) — ISBN 978-0-517-57265-8 (pbk.)
1. Children's stories, American. [1. Dogs—Fiction. 2. Death—Fiction.] I. Title.
PZ7.W64816 II 1985
[E]—19
84020060

MANUFACTURED IN CHINA
36 35 34 33 32 31 30 29 28 27

This is a story about
Elfie—the best dog
in the whole world.

We grew up together, but Elfie grew much faster than I did.

I loved resting my head on her warm coat. Then we would dream together.

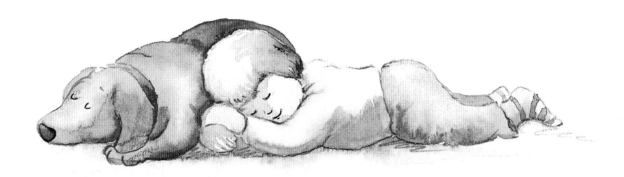

My brother and sister loved
Elfie very much, but she was
my dog.

Every day, Elfie and I
played together.

Elfie loved to chase squirrels

and to dig in my mother's flower garden.

Sometimes my folks
would get very angry
with Elfie when she
would get into mischief.
But they still loved
her, even when they
scolded her.

The trouble was, no one told her except me.

The years passed quickly, and while I was growing taller and taller, Elfie was growing rounder and rounder.

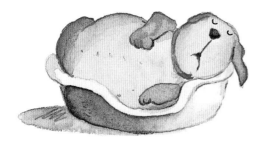
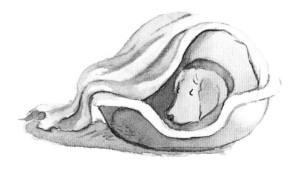

The older Elfie got,
the more she slept,
and the less
she liked to walk.
I was getting worried!

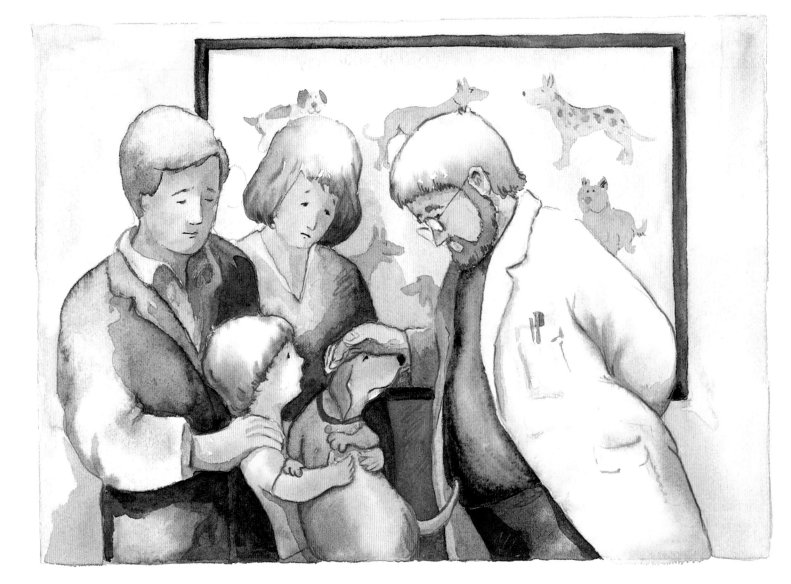

We took Elfie to the vet,
but there wasn't much he could do.
   "Elfie is just growing old,"
he said.

It soon became too difficult
for Elfie to climb the stairs.

But she *had* to sleep in my room.

I gave Elfie a soft pillow
to sleep on, and before
we went to sleep
I would say to her,
"I'll always love you."
I know she understood.

One morning I woke up
and discovered that Elfie
had died during the night.

We buried Elfie together.
We all cried and hugged
each other.

My brother and sister loved Elfie
a lot, but they never told her so.
I was very sad, too, but it helped
to remember that I had told her
every night, "I'll always love you."

A neighbor offered me a puppy.
I knew Elfie wouldn't
have minded, but I said no.

I gave him Elfie's basket instead.
He needed it more than I did.

Someday I'll have another dog,
or a kitten or a goldfish.
But whatever it is, I'll tell it
every night: "I'll always love you."